The Best of

Moral Stories

Compiled by Mrs Rungeen Singh

Young Learner Publications™

G-1, Rattan Jyoti,

18, Rajendra Place

New Delhi-110008 (INDIA)

Ph.: 25750801, 25820556

Fax : 91-11-25764396

Printed at : Kumar Offset Printers, Delhi-92

CONTENTS

THE CATTY MONKEY

Once there were two cats who were good friends.

One cat found a pancake and brought it to the other so that both of them could share it. A monkey was eyeing the pancake sitting on a tree.

The first cat divided the pancake into two equal halves and gave one half to the second cat.

But the second cat said, "You have taken the bigger piece and given me the smaller one."

Soon they were fighting over the size of the piece of pancake. The monkey climbed down the tree and interrupted them.

He said, "I will help you with the problem. You say that this piece of pancake is bigger."

The monkey took a piece and put it in his mouth. Then he compared the two halves again.

He said, "Now they are equal. Oh Lord! The two halves are still not equal." He took a big bite from the bigger one.

The two cats thought that the monkey was trying to help them solve their problem, but then they saw that the monkey kept on eating the pancake, and after a while only a little of it was left.

In the end, he finished the whole pancake and then, the cats realised that the monkey had fooled both of them. From this, the cats learnt the lesson that they should not have fought between themselves.

MORAL : ONE SHOULD NOT FIGHT WITH FRIENDS OR OTHERS WILL TAKE ADVANTAGE OF IT.

THE CLEVER CROW

A crow was thirsty and wanted to drink water. He flew around looking for water.

All the ponds of the area had dried up because it was summers, and it had not rained for many days.

The crow flew to the huts in the village to look for water. He felt very happy when he found one earthen pot lying on the ground.

But when he went near the pot, he saw that there was very little water inside it.

There was no way in which the crow could reach the water in the pot.

The crow felt like crying. He was so near the water, yet could not drink it.

Then he thought, "Crying will not help me. I have to try and do something on my own. I have to think and find a way out."

The crow thought, "If I cannot get to the water, then let the water come to me."

He wondered for some time. Then he looked around. He thought if he could raise the level of the water, then he could easily drink it. He thought and thought very hard.

Suddenly, the crow saw some small stones and pebbles lying around.

He got an idea. He thought, "If I put these pebbles inside the pot, the water will rise. Let me try. I must not give up."

The crow flew and picked up a small stone, then flew back and put it in the pot.

Then he flew back again and then again. It was hard work but the crow did not give up. Slowly, the stones and pebbles settled at the bottom of the pot and the water started rising.

The crow felt very happy. He went on working hard, by putting stones and pebbles in the pot.

Then the water slowly came up as the crow put pebble after pebble in the pot.

In this way, the clever crow was able to drink the water and quench his thirst.

After drinking the water, the crow thought, “Water has never tasted so good. It feels so nice, because it was my idea to bring the water up the pot and I have worked really hard for this water.”

MORAL : HARD WORK ALWAYS BEARS FRUIT.

THE WISE CAP SELLER

A cap seller had gone to another village to sell his caps. He could not sell many caps.

As he was walking back to his village, he began to feel very tired.

He sat down under a tree to rest and kept his bag full of caps on one side.

He was so very tired that he fell asleep almost immediately. When he got up he could not see his bag of caps.

He was very worried. He looked around. Then he saw his empty bag lying nearby. The cap seller thought, "Where are the caps? If my bag is here, then my caps must be here too."

Suddenly, he felt as if many eyes were watching him. He looked up and was very surprised.

There were many monkeys on the tree and they were all wearing his caps on their heads.

The cap seller wanted his caps back. So he shouted at the monkeys, but they did not move at all.

The poor cap seller became worried. If he didn't get back his caps, he would lose a lot of money.

So he tried shaking the tree, but the monkeys kept sitting there. The cap seller was already very tired, but he did not give up. He decided to use his intelligence to find a way out.

He sat down to rest, and started thinking of ways to get back the caps from the monkeys.

He thought, "What do I know about monkeys? I know that they eat bananas but I don't have bananas with me."

Then, suddenly an idea came to his mind. He knew that monkeys often did what they saw others doing.

They loved to imitate others. So the cap seller got up and stood in a place where he could see all the monkeys and the monkeys could see him.

Then the cap seller brought his hand over his head and caught his own cap.

He threw his cap on the ground. At once, all the copycat monkeys too threw their caps on the ground.

Quickly, the cap seller picked up his caps and ran away from there.

MORAL : DO NOT GIVE UP. THINK OUT A WAY.

THE PET MONGOOSE

A farmer lived with his wife and baby. He had a pet mongoose too.

One day his wife told him, "I have been invited to a function in the village and I have to go. Can you stay back to look after the baby?"

The farmer told his wife, "Yes, you go. I will stay at home and look after the baby."

After his wife had gone, the farmer put the baby to sleep in his cot.

All of a sudden, he heard footsteps coming quickly towards his house.

Some soldiers came and said to the farmer, "The king has summoned all the farmers for a meeting in the village. You have to come at once."

"I can't come because my wife is not here to look after the baby," the farmer replied.

A soldier said, "This is the king's order. If you don't come, the king will surely punish you."

The farmer was left with no choice but to go with the soldiers. So he called his pet mongoose and said, “I have to go. You look after the baby.”

The mongoose sat near the cot and kept a watch on the baby. All of a sudden, he felt uneasy.

He felt as if there was some danger to the baby. He looked around and saw a snake coming in through the window.

The mongoose moved quickly when he saw the snake going towards the baby.

He then pounced on the snake and both of them fought for a long time.

The snake tried very hard but the mongoose used all his strength to stop the snake from going near the baby.

The snake tried again and swung towards the baby. Now the mongoose became very angry.

He grabbed the snake by the neck and bit him hard. Finally, the snake died.

The mongoose then sat near the door waiting for his master to return. The mongoose was in pain because the snake had hurt him, but still he kept sitting till the farmer and his wife returned.

The farmer saw blood on the nose of the mongoose and started beating him with a stick.

He said, "You have blood all over your face. You must have harmed my baby."

The farmer's wife ran to see if the baby was well. Then she shouted to her husband, "Stop beating him. Come here."

The farmer went and saw the baby lying safely in his cot.

He also saw the dead snake lying near the cot, with blood all over the floor.

Then he understood that his loyal pet had saved the baby from the poisonous snake.

The farmer thanked the mongoose for saving the baby and apologised for beating him.

He said, "Forgive me. I should not have hit you. You have proved to be truly loyal. I should have checked the facts before losing my temper."

His wife also thanked the mongoose for saving the baby and gave him a special treat.

MORAL : LOOK BEFORE YOU LEAP.

THE MOVING TAIL

A crocodile and a crab were very good friends. They lived near a big lake. There were many fish in the lake and so both of them easily caught fish for their meals and never went hungry.

One day, the crocodile said to the crab, "I am fed up of eating fish. I wish we could eat something else." The crab agreed.

The crocodile continued, "All the animals are actually afraid to come to this lake because of me. So we have to eat only fish."

"It is boring to have fish all the time. Let me think. We should plan to make other animals start coming to this lake again," said the crab.

"How I wish they were not afraid of me! Crabby," sighed the crocodile.

"That is it, Crocky. Animals will only come here if they are not afraid of you," said the crab.

"How?" asked the crocodile.

"Crocky, you can go and hide somewhere," said the crab.

"That will not help at all, Crabby. There are no secrets here in the forest. Everybody here knows what is happening everywhere," said the crocodile.

"Very true. Oh! What if you were dead, Crocky!" said the crab.

"Excuse me, Crabby. I thought you were my friend," said the crocodile, getting angry.

"Come on, Crocky! I am not saying that you really die. You can pretend to be dead," said the crab.

"Well, that is possible," replied the crocodile.

"You can lie still as if you are dead and I will tell all the animals that you are dead," said the crab.

"They will still not come near me," said the crocodile.

"I will tell them that they can go near you and check whether you are dead or not. When they come near, then you can eat them," said the crab.

"I think this is a very good idea," said the crocodile.

"So let's begin now. You die, Crocky," said the crab.

"I am already dead. All the best, Crabby," chuckled the crocodile.

The crab ran out and told whoever he met that the crocodile had died and that they could safely drink water from the lake.

Then the crab met a jackal. He told the jackal about the crocodile being dead.

The jackal was thirsty and wanted to drink water. So he went with the crab towards the lake.

Meanwhile, the crocodile was ready to play his part. He lay still pretending to be dead. He was eagerly waiting for his crab friend to lure some animal into their well planned trap.

The jackal saw the crocodile lying still, but he was not sure that the crab was speaking the truth.

The jackal was very wise. He knew that the crab and the crocodile were friends.

He could not understand why the crab was not feeling bad about his friend's death.

The jackal decided to find out the truth behind the crocodile's death by playing a trick.

He said loudly, "Is the crocodile really dead, Mr Crab?"

The crab replied, "Yes, dear Mr Jackal."

The jackal said, "But when a crocodile dies, its tail moves sometimes."

The crab said, "Yes, the crocodile's tail does move sometimes. Just watch."

The crocodile had been listening to their conversation. He could no longer wait to gobble up the jackal. So when he heard about dead crocodiles moving their tails, he began to move his tail too, to convince the jackal.

Then the jackal said, “So this is just a plan to fool the other animals.”

“No, no,” cried the crab.

“Of course, it is. You are telling a lie that the crocodile is dead,” said the jackal.

“But see, he moved his tail as a dead crocodile would,” assured the crab.

“The crocodile is alive. A dead crocodile would never have been able to move his tail,” said the jackal in a loud voice.

The crab muttered, “But you said just now that a dead crocodile moves its tail.”

The jackal said, “That was just to test whether you were telling the truth. Now I will tell every animal in the forest that you both are not only cunning but liars too.”

The crab and the crocodile felt very ashamed as the jackal ran away to tell others about the lie. After this, the two friends, the crab and the crocodile, had to be content eating only fish and nothing else.

MORAL : BE SURE BEFORE TRUSTING ANYONE.

ALL FOR THE BEST

Once, the prime minister of a kingdom said, "My Lord, whatever happens, happens for the best."

The king said, "I don't agree."

Just then a strong gust of wind blew and the heavy door closed right on the king's hand with great force, and one of his fingers got cut immediately.

The severed finger fell down and the wound started bleeding profusely.

The king screamed with pain and a servant ran to call the royal doctor.

The king was in great pain for a long time and then he looked at the prime minister.

The king asked, “What do you say now?”

The prime minister replied, “I would still say that this is for the best.”

“Do you mean to say that even the loss of a finger, all this blood and this pain is for the best?” asked the king, surprised.

“Yes, my Lord,” replied the prime minister confidently.

“Mr Prime Minister, here I am in so much pain, and you say that it is for the best! How dare you?” said the angry king.

“But it is the truth, My Lord. I have full faith. Whatever happens in life, always has some good reason, even if it may appear to be a bad thing to happen,” replied the prime minister calmly.

The king was infuriated at the prime minister's words.

"Soldiers, arrest the prime minister," commanded the king.

The prime minister was put in prison, and another minister was appointed as the new prime minister.

Then one day, the king went to the forest to hunt and some dacoits saw him.

As the king and his men camped to rest, some dacoits came and surrounded them, and tied them with chains.

They took the king, the new prime minister and the soldiers to their chief.

The chief said, "You have done well to bring these people. Now we can sacrifice one of them to our Goddess."

The chief pointed at the king who looked the healthiest. The dacoits made the king stand at the sacrifice altar.

Suddenly, the chief said, "Wait. First check and make sure that this man has no cut or mark on him."

A dacoit checked and replied, "Chief, he doesn't have a finger."

"Oh! Then he cannot be sacrificed. Leave him and check the other man with him," ordered the chief.

The new prime minister was checked and found to be without any mark on his body.

So he was sacrificed by the dacoits, to please their Goddess.

Then the king and his soldiers were freed by the dacoits. The king rode to his palace at once.

The first thing he did, was to free the old prime minister who was in prison.

The king said to him, "You were right. This cut finger saved me from being killed."

"So it was for the best," said the old prime minister.

The king said, "Yes, but what benefit has come to you out of staying so long in the prison?"

The old prime minister said, "If I would have been with you and not in prison, I would have been killed instead of the new prime minister."

"You are right. I am sorry for treating you so badly. Now I am appointing you the prime minister again," said the king.

"Thank you, My Lord," said the prime minister, gratefully.

MORAL : WHAT YOU THINK IS BAD FOR YOU, MIGHT ACTUALLY BE GOOD FOR YOU.

THE PAINTING

Once a king went for hunting in the forest. As the sun began to set, he ordered his men to camp.

He loved painting, so to relax, he went onto the top of a hill to paint. He saw the beautiful sunset and decided to paint it.

He kept on painting and as soon as he had finished, he looked at the painting to see how it looked.

He went to the left and saw the painting. Then he went to the right to see whether it looked all right and perfect.

He also stepped back to see the painting. However, when the king moved back, he did not realise that he was right on the edge of the hill.

Just then, a shepherd boy, who was taking his sheep back home, saw the king standing on the edge of the hill.

He ran up the hill but the king was on the other side. The king was standing right on the edge of the hill.

The boy knew that he had to be very careful and there was no time to waste. At any moment, the king could fall off the high cliff.

The boy thought that even if he shouted, the king might get startled and lose his balance.

The boy then quickly ran and tore the painting. The king was shocked and angrily, he came towards the painting. In this way, the king's life was saved.

The king did not know that the boy had saved him from falling down the cliff. He slapped the boy hard, and shouted at him saying, "How dare you tear my painting?"

"I am sorry, My Lord, but please look behind. You were standing on the very edge of the hill," said the frightened shepherd boy.

The king looked behind and couldn't believe his eyes. If he had taken another step backwards, he could have fallen down.

The boy continued, "Yes, you could have fallen down, My Lord. So I tore the painting because then it was sure that you would get away from the edge of the hill."

The king said, "Oh! You have been very clever. I am sorry, I hit you when you have actually saved my life."

"I am sorry for tearing your beautiful painting," apologised the boy.

"Don't worry about that. I can always paint another one, but had I fallen down, it would have surely been my end," said the king.

The king walked back with the boy and then rewarded him for saving his life.

The king then told the boy that he should go to school to study, and that he would pay for it. The boy was delighted and thanked the king.

MORAL : ONE MUST THINK QUICKLY, AND FIND A WAY OUT IN TIMES OF TROUBLE.

THE FOOLISH KING

Once there was a king who did not use his brain before he did anything.

Without thinking, he would speak in his court and then afterwards, repent his words and actions.

One day, he was walking in his beautiful garden. It had rained in the morning, and the air was cool and pleasantly crisp.

The king was in a happy mood but all of a sudden, he screamed.

A thorn had pricked his foot and it was giving him a lot of pain. This made him very angry.

Then the king sent his guard to call the prime minister, who was a very wise man.

As soon as the prime minister came, the king said angrily, "You do not look after my kingdom well. Just now my foot was hurt by a thorn. It has caused me lot of pain."

"I am sorry to hear that," replied the prime minister.

"What is the use of your being sorry? It will not cure the pain of the thorn prick," shouted the king angrily.

Though a guard had taken out the thorn, the king was still in a lot of pain.

“I will call the doctor,” said the prime minister.

“That has already been done, but you are not looking after my kingdom properly,” said the king.

“I try my best, My Lord,” assured the prime minister.

“Your best is not good enough. Why was the thorn there at all?” asked the king.

“But, My Lord, what can I do about that?” asked the surprised prime minister.

The king replied, “Had there been a carpet here, I would not have hurt myself.”

“Very true, My Lord, but this is a garden,” said the prime minister.

“Cover my whole kingdom with carpets so that no one is hurt by thorns,” said the king.

“How can that be done, My Lord? It is not possible to cover every inch of this vast kingdom with carpets. It would simply not work,” replied the prime minister.

"My Lord, I have another idea. Why don't you wear leather on your feet? Then thorns won't hurt you," said the prime minister.

The king agreed happily. The prime minister, then got beautiful leather shoes made for the king. The king was pleased and no thorn ever hurt his feet again!

MORAL : SOMETIMES THE SIMPLEST SOLUTION IS THE BEST SOLUTION.

INSIDE THE TENT

It was a cold day. A trader was travelling through the desert on his camel.

As it became dark, the trader stopped to rest. He put up a tent to protect himself from the cold icy winds.

The tent was very small so the trader came in and lay down inside, while the camel was left outside.

A very strong wind started blowing and it became very cold. The camel tolerated the cold for some time.

Then he asked his master, “May I bring my head and neck inside the tent?”

The master moved to one side and said, “Yes, you may. It is cold outside.”

The camel then put his head and neck inside the tent. He sat like that for some time.

Then the camel requested his master, “May I put my forelegs too inside?”

"Yes," said the kind trader, and shifted to the corner of the tent. They sat like this for a while.

It was getting colder and colder. In spite of the tent, the trader sat with his teeth chattering.

Then again the camel asked, “Can I shift in a bit? It is very cold outside.”

The trader shifted a bit and let the camel slide in a bit more.

Then the camel said, “Half my body is outside, and I am shivering due to the cold winds. Can I come inside the tent, a little more?”

“That is true,” replied the trader, his teeth chattering with the cold wind coming into the tent. So the camel brought his entire body inside the tent.

The tent was too small for both of them. The master tried to squeeze in one corner, and seeing this the camel spread out in the small tent.

All this while, it was getting colder and colder. The wind began to blow harder and the trader pulled his robe closer to his body.

The camel then said, “I want the whole tent to myself. The tent is very small for both of us, so I stay in and you go out.”

The selfish camel then nudged his master out of the tent.

The master was amazed at the selfishness of the camel. The camel lay inside the warmth of the tent while the poor master sat outside, shivering in the cold darkness of the night.

MORAL : ONE MUST NOT BE TOO KIND OR OTHERS MIGHT TAKE ADVANTAGE.

THE PINK DRESS

Rachael was a sweet little girl who loved her mother a lot. One day her mother said, "You can go with our master and mistress, and buy a dress for yourself."

"But mother, we are so poor. How can I afford to buy a new dress when we barely have enough to eat," said Rachael.

"I have never bought you new clothes. I have saved some money to buy you a nice dress, my child," replied her mother lovingly.

"You are so sweet, Mother. Thank you so much," said Rachael.

"You go with our master and mistress. Don't keep them waiting," said her mother, who was a housekeeper in that house.

"Will I go in the car?" asked Rachael.

"Yes," answered her mother.

Rachael was very happy because she had never sat in a car before. Her father had died and her mother worked as a housekeeper to earn a living.

The master of the house, his wife and their daughter, Angie got ready to leave, and they told Rachael to sit in the car with them.

"Mom, why is Rachael coming with us?" asked Angie in an irritated tone.

"Hush child! We have to buy a dress for her," replied her mother.

"How can she sit in our car? She is poor and dirty, Mom," asked Angie.

Rachael stopped smiling and felt hurt when she heard Angie.

"Keep quiet," scolded Angie's dad.

Angie's mother then said, "Don't mind Angie's words, Rachael. You know she is a pampered child."

Now, Rachael felt better and Angie's father drove the car to the shopping area.

Rachael glanced at Angie who looked quite angrily at her. Feeling sad, Rachael turned her head and looked outside.

Soon Rachael had forgotten everything else. She looked around. The city was beautiful. Rachael had never come to these big markets before.

Then the car stopped and they went inside a shop. Rachael was surprised to see such a big shop.

"Rachael, close your mouth or a fly will get in," said Angie rudely.

Rachael exclaimed, "Isn't all this wonderful, Madam?"

Madam smiled at Rachael. Actually, she liked Rachael for she was a very well behaved girl.

Rachael and Angie were nearly of the same age, but Angie was ill-mannered.

The mother bought a lot of expensive and beautiful things for her daughter, Angie.

Then they began looking for a dress for Rachael. She liked a pink one, but it was very expensive.

Angie's mother said lovingly, "Tell me whichever dress you like. Your mother has given me a lot of money for you."

Angie interrupted, "Where did she get so much money from? She is so poor."

"She has saved to buy a dress for Rachael," replied Angie's mother.

"She must have stolen the money from us," said Angie in a rude voice.

"Keep quiet," shouted her father, as he saw Rachael's eyes fill with tears.

Angie's father came towards Rachael and asked kindly, "Rachael, which dress do you like?"

Rachael was afraid of him and she quickly pointed at the pink dress. Angie's father asked the salesgirl to pack the dress.

All of a sudden, Angie spoke out, "But I too want that pink dress."

Angie's mother tried to explain, "We have bought so many things for you, Angie. Let Rachael take what she likes." She was beginning to get tired of her daughter's demanding attitude.

"No! I want that very pink dress," persisted Angie and started shouting.

Her father looked very angry and he raised his hand to hit Angie, but Rachael said, "Sir, it does not matter. Let Angie have this dress. It would look very nice on her."

Angie's mother then said, "Rachael, you buy something else."

"No, thank you, Madam. May I ask you something?" asked Rachael.

"Yes, Rachael, you may," replied Angie's mother.

"Can we get a dress for my mother for this much money? I want to buy her a new dress. She works so hard and she never buys anything for herself," said Rachael.

"What about you?" asked Madam.

"I already have two dresses. One, I am wearing and the other one is at home. I don't need any more. Please Madam, buy a dress for my mother," requested Rachael.

Angie's mother then bought the pink dress for Angie and a lovely dress for Rachael's mother.

Rachael was very happy now. Angie's father then praised Rachael, "You are a wonderful girl. God bless you. How I wish Angie was like you."

MORAL : BE KIND TO OTHERS. DON'T BE SELFISH AND GREEDY.

THE NAUGHTY ELEPHANT

In a forest, all the elephants lived together like a family. When they walked to the lake or to search for food, they kept the baby elephants in the centre.

One day, a naughty baby elephant started walking around on his own, away from his family.

His mother got angry and said, "There are some rules and you have to follow them. So don't be naughty."

But the baby was tired of hearing his mother preach, "Don't do this," and, "don't do that," and so he did not listen to her.

In fact, the herd of elephants was going to the river to drink water.

The mother elephant advised the baby, "You must be careful. The river is deep, so stay with us."

When they reached the river, the baby elephant looked around and saw that no one was watching him. Then he quietly went into the river.

He loved the cool water but soon, the baby elephant began to scream because the fast current of the river began to sweep him away.

The baby elephant could not stand in the water any more, and he did not know how to swim.

The water carried him, and soon he saw a waterfall right in front of him.

He knew that if he fell with the waterfall, then he will surely get hurt or even die.

The baby elephant thought, "Oh! Why did I not listen to my mother? She had told me that the river was deep."

He shouted, "Help! Mom! Help! I am drowning."

The mother heard the voice of the baby. She called out to one of her sisters, "Help! My baby is drowning. Come quickly."

Both of them ran towards the baby. The baby elephant was slowly drifting towards the waterfall.

His mother shouted, "Baby, catch hold of something. Don't worry, we are coming to save you."

"Mom, help me! Please come quickly," cried the frightened baby elephant.

The mother said, "Don't cry. You must think of a way to save yourself till we reach you. Try catching hold of a big rock or something."

The baby elephant started thinking hard. He saw some plants in front of him. So instead of crying, he caught the plants with his trunk.

He kept holding on to the plants for sometime. His mother saw this and shouted, “Good boy. Hold the plants tightly, so that we both get time to reach you.”

However, they were about to reach the baby, when the plants slipped from his trunk and he was carried further away with the water.

The baby elephant tried to stay away from the waterfall but the water was too fast.

One of the elephants on the bank cried, “Do you need help?”

The mother elephant cried back, “Yes! The water is very fast. We need help.” Now all the elephants were watching them. Two other big elephants came to help them.

By then, the two elephant sisters had reached the baby.

The mother and the aunt joined their tail and trunk respectively, and stopped the baby elephant from getting swept further down the river.

Then slowly, they started pulling the baby elephant towards the bank.

It was a hard task because the water was very fast, but the other two elephants had also joined them in the rescue.

After a while, they pulled the baby elephant out of the water onto the river bank.

The two brother elephants and the sister walked off, but the mother of the baby elephant stayed with him to see whether the baby was fine.

First the mother elephant checked the baby to ensure that he was breathing properly. Then, she patted him and spoke softly to him.

When she saw that the baby elephant was smiling again, the mother slapped him with her trunk and shouted at him, "Why did you go into the water?"

"I am sorry, Mom, I was naughty," replied the baby.

"Young children have to obey rules and be disciplined. It is to keep you safe. So you must not be naughty anymore," advised his mother.

The baby said, "Never again, will I disobey you, Mother. I have learnt my lesson."

MORAL : ONE SHOULD OBEY ELDERS AND FOLLOW RULES.

GOOD FROM BAD

One day, a woman saw her baby getting very cranky. She felt his forehead and was worried to find him running a very high temperature.

She decided to take the baby to a doctor but she didn't have a car because her husband had taken it.

She started walking as there was no taxi or rickshaw around. She had to walk a long distance, and all this while, her baby was getting even more irritable.

The woman walked on with the baby in her arms, till she reached a clinic of a doctor.

She rushed inside and said, "Doctor, my baby is very sick."

The doctor examined the crying baby.

"Doctor, how is my baby? What has happened to him? He has not been eating anything, and his body feels so hot. He is even crying a lot," said the worried mother.

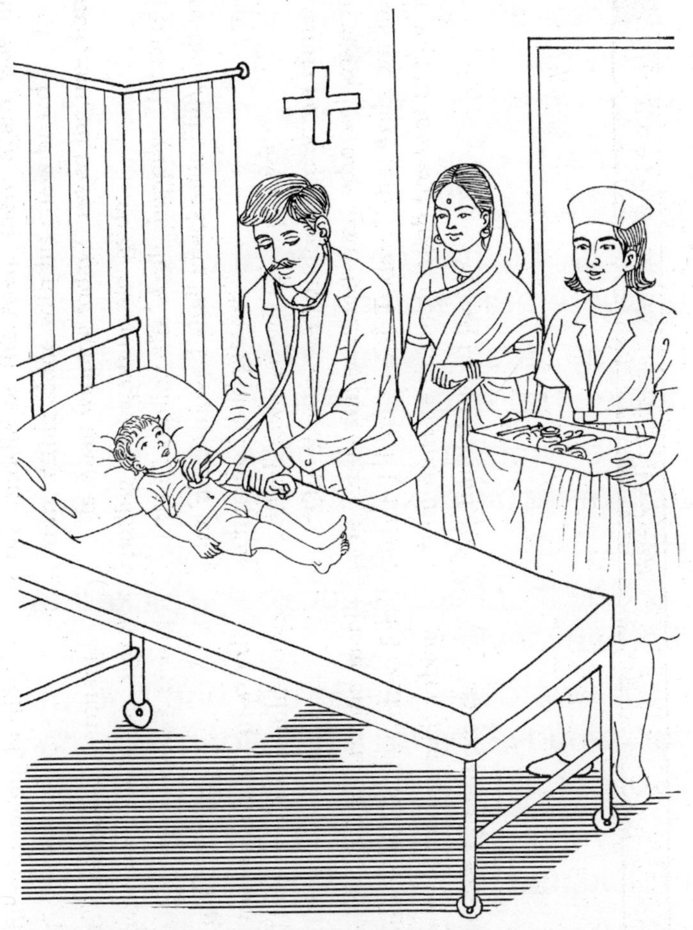

The doctor replied, “The baby has very high fever. I will have to give strong medicines and injections. You better wait here for sometime. You can take the baby home once the fever comes down.”

Throughout the day, the woman kept sitting near her baby, and it was only in the evening that the fever came down.

The doctor asked, "Have you called your husband?"

"No, he has gone to another town," answered the woman.

The doctor said, "Now you can go home. The baby is better."

He wrote a prescription and told her to give medicines to the baby at the right time.

She thanked the doctor and picked up the baby lovingly.

It was dark outside and had become very cloudy. She felt that a storm was soon to break, so she tried to hurry.

Even now, she could not find any taxi or rickshaw. So she walked on.

All of a sudden it started raining heavily. She looked around for a place where she could find shelter and saw an old temple. Keeping her baby wrapped in a blanket, she ran towards the temple.

The temple was in ruins. She sat down and made the baby sit on her lap. Suddenly, she heard a hissing sound and saw a snake right in front of her.

The woman shouted, “God! Why are you troubling me so much today?” But then she thought that she should act fast. It was still raining but she ran out of the temple with the baby in her arms. She had barely stepped out of the temple, when she heard a loud crashing sound. She turned back to find the whole temple crumbling down.

The woman thought, "Oh God! What a narrow escape for both of us. My baby and I were sitting exactly where the roof has fallen down. We would have died if we had stayed in the temple any longer."

She then knelt with her baby and prayed, "God forgive me. I shouted angrily at you when I saw the snake because I thought it would bite us. But the snake actually saved us. It made me run away, so we got saved from the falling roof. The snake was a signal for us to leave the temple. I was blaming you, but actually you were helping us. I am sorry for shouting like that. I should have kept my faith in you because you look after us all the time."

Soon the rain stopped and she walked home with the baby.

The woman reached her house safely with the baby. She thanked God again for looking after both of them, and keeping them alive.

MORAL : WHATEVER HAPPENS, HAPPENS FOR THE BEST.

THE MONKEY'S REVENGE

A boy was going to school. He saw a small monkey sitting on a low branch of a tree.

The boy picked up a stone and hit the monkey with the stone.

The small monkey screeched, “Cheeee Cheee,” because she was hurt.

The boy forgot about it and had a nice day. He studied and played in the school.

But the poor monkey was very hurt. Blood flowed from the wound and she was in a lot of pain.

With great difficulty, she reached her family. They saw the blood and her father asked, “How did you hurt yourself?”

The small monkey said, “A boy hit me with a stone.”

The mother monkey lovingly picked her up and licked the wound, till the blood stopped.

The small monkey was in terrible pain though the wound was no longer bleeding.

Her parents were furious and the father monkey decided to complain to their leader to take immediate action against the naughty boy.

Then they all went to the other monkeys of their tree. They called for a meeting.

All the monkeys sat together and the father monkey said, "A boy hit my small child today with a stone. My child has lost a lot of blood and is in much pain."

All the monkeys shouted, "Shame on the boy!"

Another monkey complained, "This boy hit my son too with a stone, sometime back."

"That is too bad. It means that this boy keeps hurting our babies," said their leader.

"I think we should take revenge," said the father of the monkey who had been hurt that morning.

"Revenge! Yes, we must take revenge," shouted all of them.

The leader said, "Revenge is not a good thing. We didn't like the boy hurting our child, but if we take revenge, we will also hurt the boy. That would not be the right thing to do."

The hurt child then said, "But Sir, this boy hits all of us every day."

All the other monkeys also agreed with what the hurt child had said.

Then, they started planning how they would take revenge.

The leader asked, “Where can we find that boy? How will we recognise him?”

“He goes to school every morning and crosses our tree on the way,” said the hurt monkey baby.

The small child replied, "I remember his face very well."

Then a plan was carefully chalked out.

They all decided to meet the next morning, at the same time the boy had hit the child with the stone.

Then they would attack the boy and beat him, so that he would never ever hurt any other animal.

The next morning, the animals quickly looked for food. Then they sat and ate their food.

They cleaned their fur and were ready to teach the naughty boy a lesson.

All the monkeys hid on the low branches of the tree, ready to attack.

The hurt monkey child sat waiting. He got confused because all the boys of the school wore the same uniform.

Her mother asked the hurt monkey, "Will you be able to recognise the boy who hurt you?"

She said to her mother, "I can never forget the boy's face."

All of a sudden, the little monkey saw the same boy coming and started shouting, “This is the boy!” The leader shouted, “Attack!”

All the monkeys who had hidden in the trees, suddenly pounced on the unsuspecting boy, and started beating and biting him.

Then the leader saw some people coming towards them, so he shouted, "Run back!"

All the monkeys ran away before the people could find stones to hit them.

In a minute, the monkeys had hidden themselves and not one of them could be seen.

The boy was lying hurt and was crying. He was taken to the doctor. He was badly bitten by the monkeys and had to take a lot of medicines.

Next day, all the monkeys waited at the same time. But the boy did not come for two days. He had fever, and had been given injections too. After two days, they saw the boy coming with a bandage on his head and stitches on his face and body. Their leader said, "We will only hurt the boy again if he throws stones at us."

The boy saw the monkeys but he did not throw even a single stone at them.

The leader shouted, “Don’t attack the boy. Let him go.” The boy just looked at them and quietly walked away. For three days, all the monkeys kept watch to see if the boy threw a stone at any monkey.

After a few days, the boy came and stood under the tree. The monkeys were again waiting for him, but were hiding themselves.

Suddenly, the small monkey, whom the boy had hurt, bravely came out of the hiding, to test whether the boy would hit again.

The boy saw the wounded monkey and apologised, "I am sorry, I hurt you. You must be in as much pain as I am. I will never hurt any animal now."

He then took out a handful of peanuts from his pocket and gave them to the little monkey.

From that day onwards, the boy never hurt any animal. The monkeys had taught him a lesson.

MORAL : WE SHOULD NEVER HURT ANIMALS.

THE LOYAL DOG

A shepherd and his family lived in a small hut, high up in the mountains. It was very cold there.

They had many sheep that grazed on the mountainside. The sheep were kept in a warm enclosure, behind their hut.

The shepherd, his wife and their baby lived on the mountains during summer. But during winters, they would come down to the village.

Once, it became cold, but they could not go down in time because the wife became sick.

It started snowing. The shepherd thought that they should go to the village, though his wife was still too weak to walk.

So the shepherd said, "I will carry you and the baby to the village."

His wife said, "I feel so weak that I can't walk. How can you carry me down? First take the sheep and when you come back, get some help to take me and the baby."

"That is a good idea. I will bring other people with me from the village, with a carry cot. You don't worry. Food is kept in the hut. I will leave the dog here and I will try to come back as soon as possible," promised the husband.

The shepherd took all the sheep with him, and started climbing down towards the village. His wife stayed back in the hut with her baby and the dog.

For a few hours, everything was quiet. All of a sudden, a snowstorm began to blow.

The wind was very strong and it blew snow everywhere for a long time.

The hut and everything else around was covered with a thick blanket of snow.

The shepherd had reached the village with his sheep, but he could not go back to his hut due to the heavy snow.

He was very worried. What would happen to his wife and baby?

He asked the other people to come with him, but they refused.

They said that the storm was too strong and they all could die if they went up the mountain.

The storm finally calmed down after a long time.

Then the shepherd started climbing up the mountain, with all the men of the village.

As they went up, they saw how strong the storm had been. All that could be seen around was snow.

When they reached the hut, they were shocked to see just a pile of wooden planks lying in place of the hut. The strong wind and snow had brought down the hut and it lay in a collapsed heap.

They could not see the woman, the baby or the dog. The man grew worried as he wondered if his wife and baby were safe.

The man started crying, "Oh! My wife and baby are not here! What could have happened to them? Where are they?"

His brother said, "Don't worry. We will find them."

They started shouting loudly for the woman and the dog.

They tried to listen for the cries of the baby.

They looked here and there and everywhere. Some started digging the snow with shovels hoping to find the woman and the baby. They called out to the baby and the woman, but no voice came, not even the baby's cry.

All of a sudden, they heard, "Woof! Woof!"

They all ran towards the side from where the sound of the dog's barking came.

Quickly, they started digging the snow. They lifted the collapsed roof of the hut carefully. They could now hear the dog's bark more clearly.

As they removed the planks of wood, they saw the woman lying with the baby in her arms and the dog covering them like a blanket. The baby and the woman were alive.

The men shouted with joy, and praised the dog for saving the woman and the baby. Quickly, they picked up the woman and the baby, put them on the carry cot and covered them with a blanket. Then all of them began their journey down the mountain, towards the village.

The dog's master then patted the dog and said, "Thank you so much. You have saved my wife and my baby. You are wonderful and truly loyal."

The others also praised the dog and patted him affectionately on his back.

It seemed the dog too agreed. He wagged his tail happily and barked in a low voice, "Woof! Woof!"

MORAL : ONE MUST BE FAITHFUL AND LOYAL TO ONE'S MASTER.

HELPING OTHERS

A long time ago, a beautiful dove lived in the deep forests. He was a happy-go-lucky fellow, and would often sit on the trees by the lake. He loved to watch the water ripple as if dancing with joy.

One day, he went to the lake feeling very thirsty. As he bent down to drink water, he saw an ant picking up some food and carrying it.

The food was heavy, so it would fall, but the ant would pick it up again and walk on. The dove thought, "What a hard-working ant! She is really great."

Just then, the dove saw the food fall off again. As the ant tried to pick it up again, she slipped and fell into the water.

The dove realised that the ant could not swim for she seemed to be drowning.

The dove felt sorry for the ant. He really admired the hard-working ant and wanted to save her from drowning. The ant was battling for her life in the swift current of the river.

The dove looked around and found a leaf lying nearby. The dove took it in his beak and put the leaf near the drowning ant.

The ant saw the leaf and tried to get on it. After much effort, she climbed onto the leaf.

The leaf floated to the side of the lake and the ant climbed out safely from the water. The ant thanked the dove.

She told the dove that she would always be there if the dove ever needed her. The ant never forgot the dove's kindness.

One day, the ant was crawling around trying to find food.

She saw a man with a gun in his hand.

The ant had seen the man kill some animals before, so she tried to see whom the man was aiming the gun at.

The ant was shocked to see that the man was aiming the gun at the dove.

It was the same dove who had helped the ant. The dove was unaware of the man, and was enjoying his food perched on a tree branch.

The ant knew that the dove's life was in danger. She had no time. She had to do something quickly to save the dove.

The ant quickly ran towards the man. She climbed up his foot as fast as she could.

The man was about to fire, when the ant bit him with all her might.

The man screamed with pain and his arms jerked suddenly.

The gun fired, but the shot missed the dove. Instead it hit the tree and no one was hurt.

The dove heard the gunshot. Before the man could fire his gun again, the dove flew away.

The man saw the dove flying into the sky but he was too busy scratching his foot, where the ant had bitten him.

By the time, the man got ready to shoot again, the dove had flown far away into the sky.

The ant felt happy that she had helped to save the dove, just like the dove had saved her when she was drowning.

After the man had gone away, the dove flew back to the ant.

He said, “I am so grateful to you for having saved my life.”

The ant replied, “My friend, I did what a true friend should do.”

They became good friends, and were always ready to help each other.

MORAL : ALWAYS BE READY TO HELP OTHERS.

THE SPIDER'S WEB

A king, with his small army, was fighting very bravely. But then he saw many of his soldiers being killed quickly.

He knew that the enemy king was stronger and mightier, and had a much bigger army than him.

He knew that because he had a small army, he would surely lose.

His soldiers had started running away from the field; this made him very sad.

He knew that he had almost lost. He turned his horse and rode off the field.

He didn't want to see anyone. So he went towards the hills. There he saw a cave. He went inside and lay down.

He felt bad as he knew that his losing this battle meant that he would lose his kingdom.

His palaces, his cities and the whole state would be taken over by his enemy. He thought of his dear queen and his sons, and his eyes filled with tears.

All of a sudden, his eyes fell on a spider spinning a web.

He knew that spiders could spin strong webs, in which insects would be caught.

It took a long time for the spider to spin a web. First, it swung from one end to another. Then it wove lines in between.

The king looked at the spider working so hard. The spider spun a very big web and then, it went to one side waiting for insects to stick to it, so that the he could eat them.

Suddenly, the king's horse neighed outside and a bird flew off near the king.

The bird's wings scraped against the web and the web was completely broken.

The king felt very sad for the spider and waited to see what he would do next.

The spider came again and started spinning all over again. This time it spun an even bigger web.

Suddenly, a gust of wind blew and the web was carried away with it but the spider remained on the wall.

Again, the king watched to see what the spider would do, as the second web had also been spoiled.

The king was surprised when he saw the spider begin to spin its web again.

The king sat up and thought, "The spider has not given up though its web has been broken twice. How brave the spider is! I should learn from him. If a small creature like a spider has not lost his will, then I, a king must not give up hope. I should not run away from my responsibilities. I will fight again."

The king got up and rode his horse. He collected all his men again and marched towards the battlefield. He was surprised to see some of his brave men still fighting. His heart was filled with a deep sense of gratitude for those loyal soldiers.

The king shouted to all his soldiers, "We have to win. We will not give up till we die." With a new found will and strength, the king and his soldiers attacked the enemy and fought a fierce battle.

The soldiers were inspired by their king's confidence. They pledged to fight and win the battle.

Even though many soldiers were hurt and killed, no one left the field. They fought till the end with a lot of courage.

In the end, the king won even though his army had been small. The other army ran away from the battle field.

All the soldiers celebrated their victory, and the king promised to give them many rewards.

All the soldiers shouted, "Long live the king! We are so lucky to have such a brave king who does not give up. Hip hip hurrah! Hip hip hurrah!"

But the king closed his eyes and thanked the spider for the lesson he had taught him. He remained grateful to the spider who had unknowingly given him the courage to face his enemies.

MORAL: SUCCESS COMES TO THOSE WHO FIGHT HARD AGAINST ALL ODDS.

THE BIRTHDAY GIFT

John was very happy that day. It was his birthday, and his father had given him some money to spend.

John thought that he would go and buy lots of books and new toys for himself. He loved to read books.

But, he felt sad that he would have to go alone because his parents were very busy.

He roamed around the market. Then he saw a thin boy of nearly his age, crossing the road. The boy tripped and fell down on the road.

He looked very pale and it seemed that the boy had not eaten for several days.

John felt a sudden rush of fear when he saw a car coming fast towards that boy on the road.

He had to do something or the boy could be killed. The car was too fast. John knew that the car would not be able to stop in time to save that boy.

John quickly jumped onto the road, pulled the boy and rolled with him onto the other side.

It was just before the car crossed over. Had John not acted so quickly, the boy would have surely been crushed under the speeding car.

All the people praised John for saving the boy, but brave John was looking at the boy.

The boy looked very weak and poor.

John said, "I am John. What is your name?"

"My name is James. Thank you John for saving me," said the boy, gratefully.

"But why did you fall on the road?" asked John.

"I don't know. Everything became dark suddenly," said James.

"Let me take you to your parents. Where do you live?" asked John.

"I don't have parents and I live on the side of this street, in that big pipe over there," answered James.

John asked, "But why?"

"My parents died in an accident two months back and I was turned out from the hut where I lived with them," replied James.

"So are you alone?" asked John.

"Yes, I am alone," answered James.

"Do you work?" asked John.

"I used to clean cars in a garage but the garage has closed down too," said James.

"Have you eaten breakfast?" asked John.

"I have not had anything to eat for three days," replied James.

John took James to a restaurant.

John said, "Come and eat, James."

"No. My mother told me never to beg," said James.

"Will you be my friend, James?" asked John hopefully.

"Yes," said James smilingly.

"Then today is my birthday. Won't you celebrate with me? If you don't eat, I will feel bad," said John.

So both of them sat down and had food. John could see how hungry James was, yet he did not eat greedily.

James said, "Thank you, John. That was wonderful."

"I am glad you liked it," said John.

"Why are you alone on your birthday?" asked James.

"My parents are very busy. Will you come with me to my house?" asked John.

"Yes," nodded James happily. Both of them walked home and James saw the house where John lived.

"You have a big house," said James.

"What is the use of a big house when I am alone most of the time? Oh! What a surprise! The car is here. That means my parents have come back," said John.

James said, "Now let me go."

But John caught his hand and pulled him along. His driver saw him and hurriedly came towards him.

The driver said, "John, your parents are looking for you. Where were you? They have arranged a birthday party for you."

John then pulled James to his room upstairs. James was quite amazed to see all the beautiful things in John's room. He had never seen anything like this ever before.

John showed him all his fancy toys and games. James played video games and was so happy that he forgot that he was not meant to be there. James had never had so much fun in his life; he was enjoying every single moment of it.

Then John took out a new set of clothes and said, "James, wear this. You are a little thin but we are of the same height. You will look very good in these clothes."

He then took him to the washroom, and asked him to bathe and wear the new clothes.

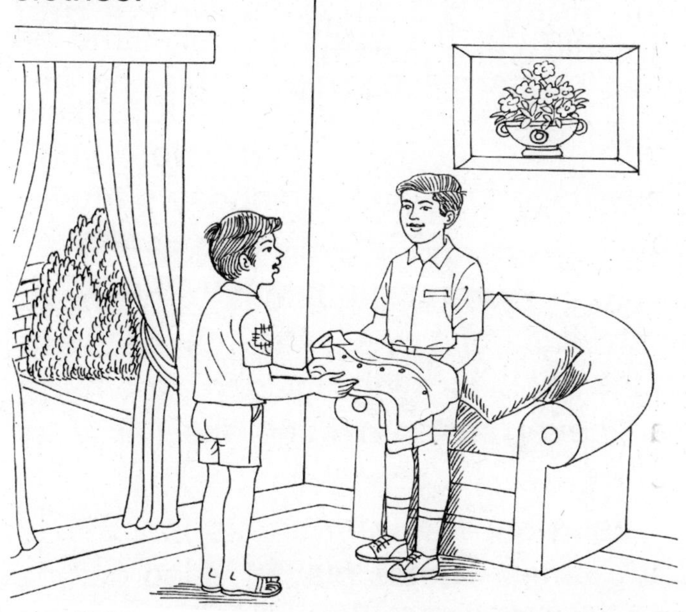

James protested, but John did not give him a chance to speak and told him to hurry up. Once James had worn the costly clothes, he looked very handsome.

John then took James down to the party. His parents hugged John lovingly and he said, "Mom and Dad. Meet my new friend, James."

Then John introduced him to all his friends. James was quite shy at first but soon made friends with them. He had a real good time with John and his friends.

John cut the birthday cake and he gave the first piece to his parents and then to James.

They danced and played games. Then John gave return gifts to his friends.

When all the guests had left, John gave one gift to James also. James changed back into his own clothes and started walking out of John's house. But John stopped him.

He took him to his parents and said, "I know you give me everything and love me a lot. Will you please give me something special today?"

His father smiled and said, "Yes, ask us for anything you want."

"You both are very busy and I remain alone at home. So, please, can James stay here with me, always?" asked John.

John told his parents all about James who was alone in this world. James was surprised when John's parents agreed to let him stay.

John jumped with joy because he had began to like James a lot.

John's mother said, "James, from today you are like my son, and you will go to school with John."

"Oh thank you so much!" said James and touched their feet in gratitude.

James and John lived happily and lovingly with their parents, ever after.

MORAL : ONE GETS MORE HAPPINESS IN HELPING OTHERS.

PAY IT BACK

The doorbell rang and the lady of the house opened the door. A boy of about eleven years of age was standing outside.

He was wearing dirty clothes and his feet were bare. His hair were dishevelled and he had tears in his eyes. He looked very poor.

The boy said, "Madam, I bring the milk bottles every day to your house."

"Oh! Yes. What do you want?" asked the lady recognising him.

"My mother is very sick and I don't have money for her medicine. Please lend me some money," pleaded the boy.

"Why don't you ask the milkman to give you money?" asked the lady.

"I did, but he did not give the money. He has also turned me out of the job," said the boy, sadly.

"I don't even know you. How can I give you money?" questioned the lady.

"Please! I promise to pay back. Please give me the money otherwise my mother might die," implored the boy.

Seeing tears in the boy's eyes, the lady felt sorry for him. So she gave him the money.

The boy thanked her and said, “I promise to return your money as soon as I can.”

The boy ran away with the money in his hand. The lady told her husband about it when he came back in the evening.

“How could you give money to someone just like that? Do you even know where he lives?” he asked his wife.

The lady replied, “The boy was so upset that I could not refuse him. He seemed to love his mother a lot.”

“These boys are good actors. I think he will never return the money,” said the husband.

The wife replied, “I am confident that he will return the money.”

However, the husband was sure that his wife had been duped by the boy.

Two months passed and the husband and wife forgot all about the money that had been given to the boy.

One day, the boy came. The lady recognised him and asked, “How is your mother now?”

The boy smiled happily and said, "Thanks to you, Madam, she is perfectly fine now. You can meet her. Mother, come here please."

An old woman appeared with a cart of vegetables and said, "Thank you very much for helping us when we needed the help. You have been very kind."

"I am glad you are well," said the lady.

"Not only that, my son used a bit of your money for buying this cart. Now he sells vegetables," said the woman.

He said, "Madam, I can return only the money, but I will never forget that you trusted me when no one else did."

"My mother was too ill at that time, and I needed the money urgently for her treatment. Even the milkman, for whom I worked, refused to give me the money, and instead turned me out of the job."

"I am so glad that I gave you the money. I knew you would return it," said the lady.

"God bless you. I hope that throughout your life you remain as honest as you are just now," she added.

The boy said with great respect, "I promise you that I will always remain honest."

"Madam, I will also help others and be kind to others as you were to me. You have taught me to have faith in others and help them in their hour of need."

He then took out some money from his pocket and gave them to the lady respectfully. Just then the lady's husband came. He met the boy and said, "You are a good boy."

"Sir, your wife is very kind," said the boy gratefully.

MORAL : ALWAYS BE READY TO HELP OTHERS AND PAY BACK YOUR DEBTS.

TRUE FRIENDS

Alex and Eric were very friendly with each other.

They had studied together right from the first standard, and had become the best of friends.

Every day they walked together to the school and back, and played together in a park in the evening.

When they came to senior school, a mean boy, Johny was jealous of their deep friendship and wanted to break it.

Johny went to Eric and said, "You, Eric, are so friendly with Alex but Alex keeps saying bad things about you."

"Really! Alex was saying bad things about me! I can't believe it," said Eric.

"You are so simple and honest. You don't understand that Alex is very bad. He is just using you," said Johny.

Eric said, "Don't say a word against Alex. He can never go against me. He is my best friend."

Johny then went to Alex and repeated, "Alex, you are so friendly with Eric, but he talks such bad things about you."

"Really! What does Eric say about me?" asked Alex, pretending to be angry.

Johny said, "Eric believes that you are dishonest and that you take advantage of his friendship."

"How dare Eric speak like that? He takes advantage of my friendship. I won't take it. I am going to tell him that I am no longer his friend," said Alex.

"So Johny will you be my best friend now? I will immediately go and tell Eric that I am not his friend any more," he asked Johny.

Johny was very happy that now Alex would fight with Eric and be his friend instead.

Alex, along with Johny, walked upto Eric and said, "So Eric, you have been speaking bad things about me. I have come here to say that I am no longer your friend."

Suddenly, both Alex and Eric turned to look at the pleased Johny and burst out laughing.

Johny was surpised and he asked, "Why are you both laughing?"

Alex replied, "We are laughing at how stupid you are. You thought that you would make us fight, but we trust each other."

Eric then explained, "No one can make us fight. We love and understand each other. I can't believe that Alex can speak ill about me. So just stop all this."

Alex added, "If we have a problem, we talk it out. We can never hurt each other. That is why we are best of friends."

Ashamed, Johny walked away.

MORAL :	TRUST YOUR FRIENDS. DON'T LET OTHERS BREAK YOUR FRIENDSHIP.

THE CUCKOO

A pretty cuckoo lived on a tree and everyone liked her for she sang very sweetly. She would sing to all the animals of the jungle and they would forget all their worries.

Once a jackal saw her and wanted to eat her. The jackal sat and planned how he could eat the cuckoo.

He then went to the cuckoo and complemented her saying, "You sing beautifully. I want to be your friend."

The cuckoo continued singing and ignored the jackal.

The jackal added, "Why don't you come down and then we can talk and be really good friends?"

The cuckoo's parents had told her to be wary of the jackal for he was very cunning.

She said, "Mr Jackal, I know you are clever but not clever enough for me."

"What do you mean?" asked the surprised jackal.

"If you want to become friends with me, then why don't you come up here on my tree? I will not come down," said the clever cuckoo.

Realising that the cuckoo was too clever for him, the jackal walked away, looking for something else to eat.

MORAL : DO NOT TRUST ANYONE BLINDLY.

THE WISE TORTOISE

A fox was hungry. He could not get anything to eat, so he went near the river which flowed through the jungle.

He saw a tortoise and ran towards it. The tortoise hid himself inside his shell.

The fox couldn't eat the hard shell and the tortoise wouldn't come out of the shell.

So the fox hit the shell against a rock but the tortoise was safe inside his shell.

The fox tried many tricks to get the tortoise out of the shell so that he could eat him.

Then the tortoise said, "I am sorry, Mr Fox, that you are having such a bad time with me."

"Come out," shouted the angry fox.

"Mr Fox, I can't come out. I am stuck in this shell. The only way is to leave me in water to soften my shell to break it easily. Then you can eat me."

The fox believed what the tortoise said, so he picked up the tortoise and threw him in the river.

The tortoise swam to the middle of the river, as fast as he could. Then he shouted, "You are stupid, Foxy. I am more clever than you."

The fox realised that he had been fooled by the clever tortoise.

The tortoise was safe in the middle of the river where the fox could not go. The fox walked away from the river looking for something else to eat.

MORAL : EVEN A CUNNING PERSON CAN BE DEFEATED BY A CLEVER MIND.

SAY 'CHEESE'

A crow was flying over a park where some people were enjoying a picnic. The food there made the crow's mouth water.

He saw the people eating many things and sat on a tree and waited.

As soon as he saw some people get up to play games in the park, the crow flew down and stole a piece of cheese.

It then flew towards the forest and sat on a tree to enjoy the cheese.

Just then, a jackal came by and saw the crow with the cheese. The jackal's mouth began to water.

The jackal said, "Dear crow. You are so lucky because you are so beautiful."

The crow felt very proud at being praised by the jackal.

The jackal continued, "You can fly high and you are also very clever."

The crow felt really happy, but then the jackal said, "But I feel very sad that you can't sing."

To prove the jackal wrong, the crow started singing and the piece of cheese fell from his mouth, on the ground below. The jackal quickly gobbled up the cheese and walked away. The crow was left behind, with his mouth gaping wide.

"If only I had been more sensible." thought the poor crow.

MORAL : DON'T BE TAKEN IN BY FALSE PRAISE.

UGLY OR USEFUL

A tortoise was always sad. She felt that she was not good looking. She was ashamed of her slow pace and small size.

She hated her shell because she thought that it made her look ugly. She mostly kept to herself, and her only friend was the frog.

One day she told the frog, "I am useless. I am fat and ugly. All the animals make fun of me and my shell. They laugh when they see me walking."

The frog said, "Everyone has something good and nice about them. No one is useless. Don't be upset because of others; no one is perfect. Let them do what they want. You should be confident of yourself."

"I am nothing compared to the others. Everyone is better looking than me," said the tortoise sadly.

"Listen, you should be proud of what you are. You should never look down upon yourself," said the frog.

"Just look at this horrible shell that I have to carry on my back," said the tortoise in despair.

Suddenly, they heard a horse galloping towards them.

The frog jumped into the water to save himself. But the tortoise could not escape and the horse ran over the tortoise.

The frog screamed with fright, "Tarrrr tarrrr. The tortoise must have died."

It came out of the water and rushed towards the tortoise, who had disappeared into his shell.

Suddenly, the tortoise came out. She was alive and well. Nothing had happened to her.

"See how lucky you are that you have a shell. If the horse had stepped on me, I would have surely died. But it stepped on you and nothing happened to you, because of your strong shell," said the frog.

"Very true," replied the tortoise.

"Now don't ever think that you are useless. Think well of yourself. Be proud of this shell which is so strong that it could save you from a horse," said the frog.

"You are right, Froggy. I will never be ashamed of my shell," realised the tortoise.

"I am glad, my friend, that you realise how useful your shell is," said the frog.

"I shall never hate myself and my shell again. It has indeed saved my life. Now I have confidence in myself, and will always remain happy with whatever I have," said the tortoise happily.

The frog looked at his dear friend and smiled.

MORAL : BE HAPPY WITH WHAT YOU HAVE.

SMALL AND BIG

Sam was lazing under a tree, enjoying the beauty of nature. He loved the green earth, the blue sky and the cool wind.

He looked up at the tree. It was huge but it had small apples growing on it.

Sam thought, "How funny! The tree is so big but the apples are so small."

Then he looked around. He saw some creepers on the ground. They had huge pumpkins growing on them.

"How funny! The pumpkins are so big but the creeper is so thin that it is growing on the ground."

Sam wondered at the ways of nature and how things were planned in the world.

He felt that since God has made everything, there must be a good reason for these strange things.

Just then an apple fell on his head. He got a tiny bump on his head and he thought, "Thank God, it was only an apple that fell on my head. If a pumpkin had fallen on my head, I could have died."

Sam thought, “Ah! That is why a big tree has small fruits and the big fruits grow on the ground. Nature has planned everything so well.”

MORAL : THERE IS A REASON BEHIND EVERYTHING IN NATURE.

A FAILED WINNER

Michael came home from school. He was crying.

"Why are you crying?" asked his worried father.

"I have failed in my English test," replied Michael.

"Don't worry, Michael. This is just one test. Work hard and get more marks next time," said Michael's father, hugging his dear son.

"But I have failed. I am not worthy of your love and affection," said Michael.

"Listen Michael. In spite of your low grades, you are still an obedient son and a good person," explained his father.

"You have not done well in just one subject. That does not make you bad," convinced his mother.

"Don't worry," his father added.

"Thank you father. I promise that I will try my best so that next time, I do not fail," said Michael feeling a little better.

"No, Michael. Just work hard and don't think about passing or failing," advised his father.

Michael then understood and said, "Thank you papa and mummy for being so understanding. I won't cry now but I promise to study hard from today."

MORAL : DON'T GIVE UP; WORK HARDER IF YOU FAIL.

AND GOD SPOKE...

Susan shouted at her mother, "You never buy good things for me. All the children have such good toys."

"But you already have so many beautiful dolls and toys. Now come on, eat your food," said Susan's mother.

"No, I will not eat. You cook potatoes all the time, and I hate potatoes. My rich friends eat such wonderful things," complained Susan.

"We are lucky that we are getting something to eat. You should eat everything," explained Susan's mom.

"There are so many poor people who have nothing to eat. Come on eat whatever is given to you," her mom added.

"I won't eat! won't eat! and I won't eat!" shouted Susan.

She saw tears in her mother's eyes. Susan ran to her bedroom and banged the door behind her. She felt that no one cared for her and lost in these thoughts, she dozed off.

Suddenly, she heard a voice, “Susan, I am God. Do you know who your mother is? I could not come to you, so I sent her to you. She loves you and cares for you. She looks after all your needs and your health. She tries very hard to keep you and others happy, but you were very rude to her just now.”

“Yes, I was rude,” confessed Susan.

“You made her cry,” said God.

“Yes, I made her cry,” said Susan, in a guilty voice.

“Was that a nice thing to do?” asked God.

“But she gets after me to eat everything,” replied Susan.

“That is because she loves you and wants to teach you the right things,” explained God.

“She always scolds me,” complained Susan.

“That is only to stop you from doing wrong things. If a child stands next to a well, won’t you shout at him to get him away from the well?” asked God.

“Well, that is true,” replied Susan.

“Parents look after their children and teach them good habits and manners. But you shouted at your mom,” said God.

“I am sorry, God,” said Susan.

“That is fine, but how will she know that you are sorry? She is crying in her room,” said God.

"I will go to her," replied Susan.

Susan suddenly woke up and thinking about her dream, she went to her mother. She said, "Mom, I am sorry for being rude. I promise never to be rude ever again. I am hungry. Can I please get food to eat?"

Mom laughed and kissed Susan wondering all along as to what had brought the change in her daughter.

MORAL :	OBEY YOUR PARENTS. THEY KNOW WHAT IS BEST FOR YOU.

TUMMY TROUBLE

The hands said to the feet, "Did you hear the doctor? He said that the stomach should be kept in a good condition."

"We do such a lot of work. Why is so much importance being given to the stomach alone?" asked the legs.

"I think we should teach the stomach a lesson," the mouth added.

The heart interrupted, "But the poor stomach has not said anything to us."

The teeth then said, "You, dear heart, are also given a lot of importance, so you are speaking in favour of the stomach."

The heart tried to explain, "No! All of us work together. I work with the brain and the lungs. We all work together and each one of us is equally important."

"But we are never given importance," complained the throat.

The feet added, "All of us work hard, but it is always the stomach, heart and the brain that everyone praises. This is most unfair."

"I will not work from today."
"I will not chew food again."
"I will no longer swallow the food."
"I will not pick up the food and put in the mouth."
"Why is so much importance being given to the stomach?"
"Stop fighting! All of us work together."
"Gosh! What has gone wrong with all my friends?"

"I will not work from today," said the tongue.

"I too will not chew the food from today," added the teeth.

"I will not pick up the food and put it in the mouth," said the hand with its fingers nodding.

"I will not swallow the food," followed the throat.

The poor stomach got no food inside when no one worked for it.

Slowly, everyone started feeling weak. Then the brain asked, "What are you doing stomach dear, this body will die."

"What can I do, dear brain. These people give me no food," replied the stomach.

Then the brain convinced everyone to work like before and soon food started coming into the stomach.

The stomach broke the food down and gave energy to the body. Now slowly, everyone began feeling better and healthier.

The throat then regretted, “I am sorry, stomach, for being jealous of you.”

The tongue added, “You are very important. You give energy to the entire body.”

Then the stomach explained, “We all are equally important. All of us have to work together to keep the body alive and healthy. Each and every part of the body has some significance. If the hands do not pick up the food and put it into the mouth and if the teeth do not help in chewing the food, then how can the throat swallow it?”

“Similarly, if the throat does not swallow the food, how can I break the food into carbohydrates, proteins and fats, and give energy?”

The tongue nodded and everyone agreed that each and every part of the body is important. They did away with their differences and began to work together again, to keep the body healthy and happy.

MORAL : ONE SHOULD LOVE ONE ANOTHER AND WORK TOGETHER.

THE PROUD DONKEY

A statue maker made a beautiful idol of God to be placed in the village temple. It took him many days to make it and he was very proud of his work.

As it was very heavy, the man borrowed a donkey from the friendly washerman and placed the idol on it.

All the people who saw the idol, bowed before it with folded hands as a mark of respect to God.

The donkey thought that all the respect was being shown to him and began feeling very proud.

He started braying out loudly as if to acknowledge the respect, people on the road were showing to it.

The idol maker who was walking with the donkey admonished him and said, "Keep quiet. If you lift your head like this to bray, the idol might fall."

But the donkey thought that the statue maker was jealous and kept on braying, "I am the best."

They reached the temple, and after placing the idol on the pedestal, the idol maker hit the donkey hard with a stick. The donkey felt the pain and saw the people bowing before the idol. He then realised that all along the way, the people had been bowing before the God. He hung his head in shame and quietly went back home with the statue maker.

MORAL : ONE SHOULD BE WISE OR ONE CAN BE PUNISHED.

THE THREE AXES

A woodcutter climbed a tree by the side of a river. He started chopping the biggest branch of the tree.

As he was cutting, his wooden axe fell into the river. The poor woodcutter felt very sad for he earned his living by selling the wood cut from the trees in the forest.

He had no money to buy another axe. So he jumped into the river and tried to look for his axe.

After a long time, he came out of the water. He was very upset because he had not found his axe.

God felt bad that such a hard working man was looking so sad. He sent his angel to help the woodcutter.

The angel saw the woodcutter sitting by the river and crying loudly. He felt pity on the poor woodcutter.

The angel decided that he would test the honesty of the woodcutter and then help him as God had wanted him to.

The angel came out of the river and said, “Dear woodcutter. I know that you have lost your axe. Take this axe.”

The angel showed the woodcutter a silver axe but the woodcutter said, “This is not mine.”

"So what? This silver axe is expensive. It will help you," said the angel.

"I am a woodcutter and I need an iron axe. Moreover, how can I take something which is not mine?" asked the honest woodcutter.

The angel again went inside the water and this time came out with a golden axe, and offered it to the woodcutter.

But the woodcutter refused saying, "This golden axe is not mine. I can't take it."

The angel then went down again in the water. This time he came out with the woodcutter's axe.

The woodcutter was overjoyed and he said, "Oh, thank you! This is my axe. I can take this. Thank you for finding it."

The angel said, "God had sent me to help you, but I wanted to test you for your honesty. So I offered you the silver and golden axes. However, you are not a greedy man. I am very happy with you."

"You are very honest. Take all these three axes. It is a reward for your honesty," the angel added. The woodcutter happily took the three axes and thanked the angel.

MORAL : HONESTY ALWAYS PAYS.

'I CAN DO IT'

Sara was a sweet little girl who had a smiling face. But her parents were very sad for their darling daughter.

This was because Sara could not walk. A small accident two years back had disabled her legs.

She would often daydream and imagine that she was running, walking and dancing with kids of her age.

She felt very sad for she couldn't walk, run or dance ever again.

One day, her parents took her to a doctor, for a check up.

Sara said, "Doctor, I am very afraid that I will never walk."

The doctor explained, "Listen to me, Sara. We should never give up in life. Those who fear nothing are brave people. And if we smile through our difficulties, God gives us strength to tide over them because he helps only those who help themselves."

Sara said, “I try to be happy even if I have pain.”

“Good girl. I think that you can walk again,” said the doctor.

“What! Oh, that would be wonderful!” said Sara, clapping her little hands.

“But you need to be confident of yourself,” said the doctor.

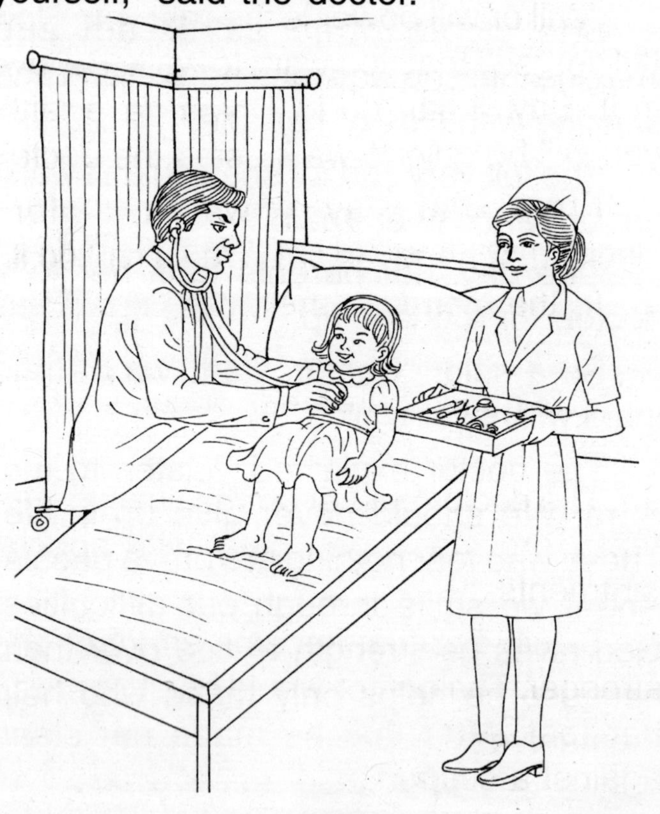

"How?" asked Sara.

"Tell your mind that it has to get your legs walking again," replied the doctor.

"How can I do that?" asked Sara.

"Your will power can make your mind do anything," replied the doctor.

"What is will power?" asked Sara.

"Will or will power is the real you. Now tell yourself that you want to walk. Believe in it. Say, 'I can do it.' If you have faith, you will be able to walk," said the doctor.

From that day onwards, before sleeping, Sara would say, "Yes. I can do it."

In the morning, she would again say to her mind, "Yes. I can do it."

She remembered her doctor's words and hoped to walk again.

The doctor put her on medication. Her feet were massaged daily with special ointments.

Slowly her feet became stronger and stronger. The doctor would often exercise her feet. After that he made her stand against a support.

One day, the doctor took away his hands from Sara and she remained standing. Everyone was very happy and little Sara clapped her hands happily. Her parents kissed her.

The doctor would then make Sara stand for a longer time each day.

Sara would get tired, but she would say to herself, “I can do it. I have to do it.”

Slowly, she learnt to stand. Then she could move her feet. Then one day, the doctor made her walk.

First, he held her and slowly made her put her right foot forward and then the left.

When he removed his hand from hers, Sara fell down.

The doctor then said, “You can rest a while, Sara.”

“No, please doctor. I have to walk,” said Sara, excitedly.

She went on trying. She held on to a railing and tried to walk.

She fell many times, but her doctor or her parents would pick her up, and she would try again.

Then one day, she could take her first step on her own. Everyone danced with joy.

Sara did not stop. Every day, she would tell herself, “I can do it,” and then try again.

After a few weeks of persistent efforts, she could walk a few steps without any help.

Finally, she could walk on her own like any other child.

Sara loved it. She was walking. She laughed and then she cried.

Her parents held her and kissed her lovingly. Sara hugged her parents and said, "I am so happy."

Then the parents walked with her to the doctor and her father said, "Doctor, thank you so much. We will never forget what you have done for us."

"By making Sara walk, you have given us life," said her mother with tears of joy streaming down her cheeks.

"I have not made Sara walk. Sara has made herself walk. She has proved how brave she is. She never said that she could not do it. She was always trying more and more and that is why she could walk," explained the doctor.

Sara said, "Thank you for saying that, Doctor, but you were the only one who told me that I could walk. You also taught me how to think in a positive manner. Thank you for that, Doctor."

She now goes to school and plays games like other children. She has made many friends and is very popular with her teachers.

She has learnt dancing. She also performs at her school functions and wins many prizes. She has fulfilled her dream with her hardwork and confidence.

MORAL : ONE SHOULD BE BRAVE AND WORK HARD, THEN ONE CAN ACHIEVE ONE'S DREAM.

BE HAPPY

Suzy was now in the fourth standard, and on the first day of the new class, she went to her new classroom. She saw that the other students had not yet come in.

Suzy saw a girl sitting in the class. She looked very sad.

Suzy went to her and said, “I am Suzy. Why do you look sad?”

“No one loves me,” replied the girl.

“Oh! But first tell me your name,” said Suzy.

“My name is Christine. Does your family love you, Suzy?”

“My family? Why don’t you tell me about your family, Christine?” asked Suzy.

“My father is a businessman. My mother is a housewife. I have an elder brother,” replied Christine.

“You said no one loves you. Do they beat you?” asked Suzy.

Christine looked up and shook her head.

"No, but mom does not give me all that I want. Yesterday, I told her to buy me shoes, but she refused," said Christine unhappily.

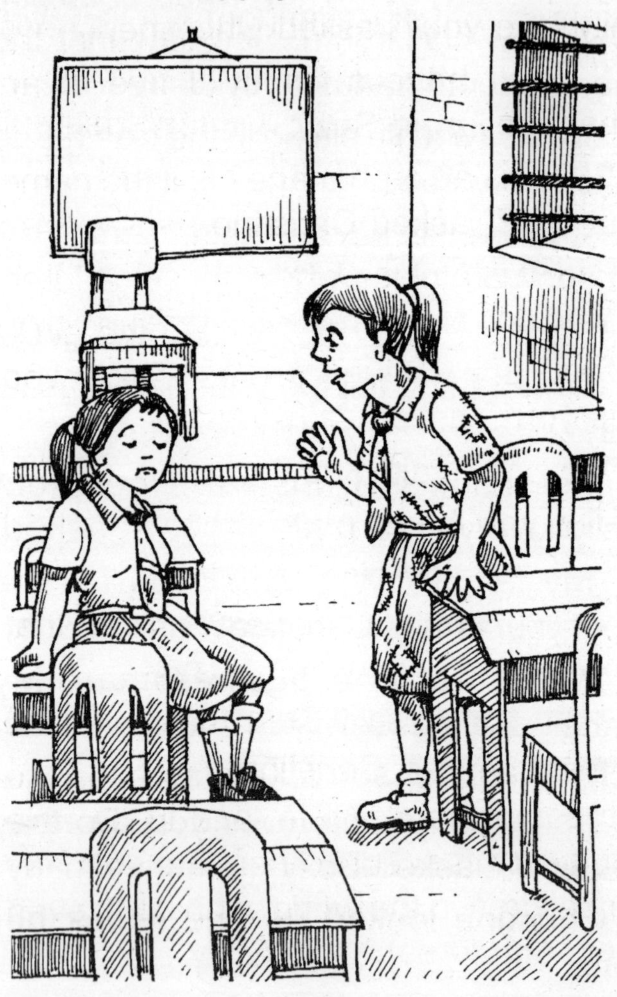

"Don't you have shoes?" asked Suzy.

"Oh I have many shoes, but I don't have pink ones, and mom refused to buy them for me. Now tell me. Does your family love you?" asked Christine.

"I don't have a family. I live in an orphanage," said Suzy.

"What is an orphanage? Is it the name of a hotel?" asked Christine.

"No, it is a place where those children live who don't have parents," replied Suzy.

"You don't have parents. Then who loves you?" asked Christine.

"No one," said Suzy.

"Do you have pink shoes?" asked Suzy.

"I have only this one pair of shoes that I am wearing," answered Suzy.

"I am sorry," said Christine.

"But I am not sorry. I am so happy to have somewhere to live, and to be able to study in this school. There are so many poor children in the world, who don't even get enough to eat," said Suzy.

Then many other girls came in and waved at Suzy. Suzy started talking and laughing with them. Christine could see how friendly she was with everyone.

Christine prayed, "Dear God, I have just realised how wrong I was. Suzy has nothing, not even a family or a house, yet she remains so happy."

"I have everything, a family, a house and my family loves me a lot. I don't appreciate what I have, and yearn for what I don't have."

"Now I will not trouble mom for new toys and pink shoes. I will ask her to give them to those who really need them. I will think of others and not just myself. I will always cherish what you have given me. Please make me strong. Amen!"

Christine was a changed person from that day, and was ever ready to help others. Suzy was glad that her new friend was happy and soon they became the best of friends.

MORAL : ONE SHOULD BE CONTENT WITH WHAT ONE HAS.